To Miss Frederica Dampier,
with love from Lizzie

Text copyright © 1996 Elisabeth Beresford
Inside illustrations © 1996 James Mayhew
Cover illustrations © 2001 James Mayhew

First published in Great Britain in 1996
by Macdonald Young Books
This edition published in 2001 by Hodder Children's Books

The rights of Elisabeth Beresford and James Mayhew to be identified as the author
and illustrator of this work have been asserted by them in accordance with the
Copyright, Designs and Patents Act 1988.

10 9 8 7 6 5 4 3 2 1

A Catalogue record for this book is available from the British Library

ISBN 0 340 79518 2

Printed by Wing King Tong, Hong Kong

Hodder Children's Books
A Division of Hodder Headline Limited
338 Euston Road, London NW1 3BH

ELISABETH BERESFORD

Lizzy
Fights On

Illustrated by JAMES MAYHEW

Hodder
Children's
Books

a division of Hodder Headline Limited

Chapter One

Lizzy was sitting on Miss Damps' garden gate waiting for the bus to come. Lizzy's mother was coming to stay for the weekend and Lizzy felt so cheerful she was trying to teach herself to whistle. But no matter how hard she puffed and blew nothing happened. Lizzy's face just got redder and redder.

It was wartime and when Lizzy's home was hit by a bomb she was sent to stay with old Miss Damps in the country while Lizzy's mother carried on working in Brighton. Lizzy and Damps had become the best of friends and they had shared some pretty hair raising adventures. But as Damps said – there was really no point in worrying Lizzy's mother about it so they kept quiet…

There was a fighter plane zooming about overhead so Lizzy never even heard the bus when it *did* arrive.

"Lizzy what are you doing?"

It was Lizzy's mother. She was really looking quite smart because she had cut out the best bits of two old dresses and turned them into an almost new dress. She was very clever at doing things like that. This was just as well as clothes were rationed – which meant you needed clothing coupons as well as money to buy clothes. Everyone had the same number of coupons but somehow Lizzy and her mother never had enough to last now that Lizzy was growing so fast.

"Waiting for you," said Lizzy.

And then she had to dive after Popeye, Miss Damps' dog, who had decided to chase after the bus. He was always chasing after things and Lizzy and Damps hoped that one day he would chase after a rabbit and they could have rabbit stew again.

"You're looking very well," said Miss Damps.

She was waiting for them at the front door wearing her old skirt and the cardigan which always had things in the pockets. Today it was some biscuits which Miss Damps had made, but they were so hard even Popeye couldn't eat them.

Lizzy went off into one of her dreams,
picking up a word here and there.

"...suddenly got a letter out of the blue
saying that Ian might be in an Italian Prisoner
of War Camp. I couldn't believe it. I still
can't..."

"Mustn't raise your hopes too high, my
dear. Another sandwich?"

"No thank you," said Lizzy's mother
politely. The sandwich filling was home-made
blackberry jam and it was a bit like toffee.

"Who is a prisoner?" asked Lizzy.

There was a moment's silence and then Lizzy's mother said gently,

"We think it might be Daddy. You know he was a soldier who went away to fight and then we didn't hear from him any more. He just seemed to— to vanish. Well now I've had a letter which says he may have been captured and put into a Prison Camp - in Italy where he was fighting... If he is there at least he'll be safe. One day he might even come back to us."

Lizzy frowned. She could hardly remember her father. He was just some rather blurred photographs and a voice. He had gone away to be a soldier when she was very young. Long before the silent bomb had hit their house. But then she remembered something else.

"He could whistle!" she said.

Her Mother said something in a rather shakey voice and Miss Damps started talking about the blackberry jam.

"We cooked it a lot," said Lizzy. Her mother was such a good cook and Lizzy wanted to be just like her one day.

"Perhaps you cooked it too much," said Lizzy's mother trying to get the spoon out of the jar. She tugged quite hard and the handle bent right over.

"Oh Damps I'm sorry," she said, "and it's real silver!"

"Doesn't matter," said Miss Damps, "I've got plenty more of them somewhere. Well next time we'll know better, won't we Lizzy?" and she gave her a wink.

As usual the weekend went far too fast and it wasn't until the noisy little bus came grumbling up the lane that Lizzy's Mother said:

"Wouldn't it be wonderful if Daddy *did* come home one day?"

"Rather," said Lizzy. "He could teach me to whistle and then Popeye wouldn't go running off everywhere because I could whistle him back!"

Which would have been very
useful the very next evening
when Miss Damps was
going round her apple trees
picking up the drops and
stuffing them into her
cardigan pockets. The
butcher's van went bumping down
the lane and Popeye suddenly went mad.
Perhaps he caught a whiff of meat. Anyway he
jumped up and down barking and then –
amazingly for a dog of his age – he scrambled
over the gate and set off after the van.

"I'll get him," said Lizzy and away she went
trying to whistle and run at the same time.
Luckily the van was so old it wasn't going too
fast. Popeye jumped up and down barking
furiously and the butcher's boy – who was
actually a very old man – shook his fist at him
and then threw a bone out of the window.

Popeye caught it and went prancing off underneath a barbed wire fence. Lizzy went after him. The driver shouted something, but she didn't hear what it was. Popeye came to a stop making terrible gasping noises and Lizzy went down on her knees to get *her* breath back. Somebody shouted at her very loudly.

"STAY WHERE YOU ARE!"

Lizzy and Popeye looked round and there, coming towards them very slowly, was a soldier with a white face.

"Put your feet *just* where I put mine," he said to Lizzy, "and I'll take the dog." And he slung a furious Popeye over his shoulder. Popeye growled, but he couldn't bite because he was hanging on to the bone.

It was only a few steps back to the wire fence, but once they were on the other side the soldier sat down as if he had walked ten miles.

"Don't you ever do that again," he said croakily, "can't you *read*?" And he pointed at a rather battered old sign.

"Course I can!" said Lizzy. "Keep out. MINES. Oh!"

"That means sort of bombs buried in the ground, see? We put 'em there when we thought the Germans might be coming over with their soldiers. I think most of 'em have been taken away now, but you can't be too careful. All right, then?"

It seemed a lot of fuss about nothing to Lizzy, still perhaps it might be better to keep quiet about it...

"All right," she said and set off home with Popeye at her heels. "Better not tell Damps," she said. And they didn't.

Chapter Two

"It says here," said Miss Damps at breakfast, "that there's going to be a Scrap Metal Drive in the Village Hall."

She looked over the top of the local newspaper, which was only four pages these days because of the paper shortage.

"Drive where?" asked Lizzy.

"I think it means that we have to collect up old bits of metal and take them along to the Hall. Then they get taken away and made into tanks and guns and planes. And there's a wonderful Surprise Prize for whoever collects the most."

"Ah!" said Lizzy. She liked surprises. Nice ones that is. Not fields with mines in them or silent bombs.

Miss Damps got out the old pram which she used when she was collecting firewood. They put a wooden box in it, Lizzy pulled on her beret and she was ready. She practised whistling as she went off down the lane and just for a moment she thought she could almost remember her father and then he vanished again.

People were very kind when Lizzy and Popeye knocked on their doors, but they had hardly any old scrap metal to give her. Old Albert at the end of the lane found a very heavy, rusty old mincer.

"Nothing to mince in it these days," he said and then winked and added in a whisper, "except a nice bit of chicken eh? Tell Miss Damps I may be round with something special for your Sunday lunch."

That meant one of Albert's chickens. Lizzy beamed. The weekly meat ration for Damps and herself was half a pound of mince and two chops so quite often they had one of Damps' rather unusual vegetable pies for their lunch.

Further on Lizzy collected a tin kettle with holes in it, a very rusty tin bath and a heavy doorstop which made the pram wheeze on its hinges.

"The trouble is," said the woman who gave it to her, "we've had so many of these scrap metal dos there's hardly anything left. And I don't see how you could make that into a bit of a plane. It'd never get off the ground.

By the end of the week Lizzy had quite a pile of metal bits and pieces, but she'd seen what the other local children had collected and they'd got more than she had. And she did so want that Surprise Prize.

And then she remembered how Miss Damps was always saying that she must sort through the rubbish in the old trunk in the cupboard under the stairs. Lizzy would do it for her! Two jobs in one. Miss Damps had gone off to do the weekend shopping – something to go with Albert's chicken. It was Lizzy's chance and she took it.

She pulled out the trunk and opened it up. It was full of bits of black metal all wrapped up in dusty old paper. Dishes and bowls, enormous plates and small trays. All of them very dirty. Miss Damps would be glad to be rid of them. Carefully Lizzy loaded them into the pram which sank down on its wheels. The things were very heavy.

Lizzy squeaked and creaked up to the Village Hall where a rather bossy woman in an overall just dumped everything onto a weighing machine, scribbled something on a piece of paper and then emptied the lot behind more loads of metal.

"The prize?" said Lizzy hopefully.

"Not now," the woman said, "come back tomorrow. Next?"

She looked so tired and cross that Lizzy fairly scuttled home. She couldn't wait to tell Miss Damps what she had done. But when she did Miss Damps went a funny colour, rather as the soldier had done, and sat down on the nearest chair.

"You took...you took everything out of the trunk?" she said at last.

"Yes, it was ever so old and dirty and heavy. I think we'll win the Surprise Prize."

"Ah," said Miss Damps. She sounded very strange, "My grandmother's old silver. It would deserve to win. I think, Lizzy, we had better try and get it back rather quickly."

Lizzy felt that this time she'd done something really wrong, but what was it? What did Miss Damps mean about her grandmother's old silver? She followed Miss Damps out of the house with Popeye at their heels. Miss Damps was pushing the pram and she had her hat on back to front.

Luckily for them it was old Albert, in his Home Guard uniform, who was just closing up the hall. He listened to Miss Damps with his mouth open and then threw back the door and pointed. There was a small mountain of junk in the hall. Bicycles with wheels missing, lawn-mowers with no handles, saucepans, bowls and kettles.

"Enough to make our very own spitfire," Albert said proudly.

Popeye went to have a look, his tail wagging like a flag. Miss Damps just stood there with her hand over her mouth.

"I'm sorry," said Albert, "But I'll have to put up the blackout in a few minutes. Perhaps if you come back tomorrow…"

Popeye was already vanishing into the gloom of the metal mountain, puffing and sniffing at an ancient oven. It was then that Lizzy got her second idea of the day. She scooped all the dusty remains of the wrapping paper out of the pram and went to kneel by Popeye.

"Find," said Lizzy firmly, putting the paper under his flat, black nose. "Find and you can have the biggest bone EVER!"

Popeye looked at her, sniffed the paper, growled deep in his throat and began to scuffle his way to one side of the metal mountain.

Half an hour later in the dusk Miss Damps,
Lizzy, Albert and Popeye wheeled their way
down the lane. The pram was full again.

"He should have been a bloodhound," Miss
Damps said proudly.

"I'm sorry," said Lizzy in a small voice. She couldn't help thinking about the Surprise Prize which was gone for ever now.

"You weren't to know that was my grandmother's old silver," said Miss Damps. "So never mind, we've got it all back. Albert you deserve a beer. And tomorrow I'll tell you about *my* idea for how we're going to win!"

27

Chapter Three

Miss Damps' idea of how to win the Scrap Metal Drive was really very simple. She gave her old car. It had been in the leaking garage since the start of the war. It had been rained on and the rats had eaten some of the seats. The salvage men who came to take it away on the back of an ancient lorry thought it was wonderful.

"It was old when I bought it," said Miss Damps, "It cost about £20 I think…"

There was quite a crowd in the Village Hall and right from the start it was obvious who was going to be the winner.

"Miss Damps and Lizzy," announced the Judge and everybody clapped.

"You collect the prize, Lizzy," whispered Miss Damps as the Judge reached under the table and produced a brown paper bag. Lizzy went up to the platform and there was a moment's silence as the Judge took something out of the bag.

"The Surprise Prize!"

It was like a very big, curved sausage and it was yellow. Everybody gasped and then they began to clap and shout and roar with laughter. Lizzy just stared. She'd seen drawings of this thing in books and perhaps long, long ago she had seen a real one. It was... it was...

"It's a banana," said the Judge. "Don't eat it all at once Lizzy or you might be sick."

There was more laughter and Lizzy went back to Miss Damps not sure if she was pleased or not with her Surprise Prize. It smelt quite nice, but did she *have* to eat it?"

"Put it in the larder," said Miss Damps. "Long ago when you were quite small you could buy as many bananas and oranges and lemons as you wanted. But they grow in hot countries and now there's a war on ships have to carry more important things..." And she sighed.

It was a bit of a let down, but almost at once there was something else to think about. The Jumble Sale in the Church Hall. Lizzy still felt a bit worried about nearly losing Miss Damps' silver and not being really pleased about the Surprise Prize. She counted up all her money and went off to the Church Hall with Popeye. It was very, very crowded and she had to duck under people's elbows to get to the second-hand clothes stall. Because clothes were rationed and in short supply people would buy practically anything.

Lizzy knew exactly what she wanted to get Miss Damps as a present. A cardigan. People kept grabbing at things over her head, but Lizzy wormed her way through everything until right at the end of the table she found it. A very large purple cardigan which looked as good as new. AND it had really big pockets. Just right for carrying apples.

It cost four shillings and nine pence which seemed a lot, but luckily Lizzy had five shillings. She was so pleased with herself that she very nearly managed a whistle on the way home.

Miss Damps was busy at the sink trying to clean some of the rescued silver. It looked a lot better now it was no longer black.

"I've got a present for you," said Lizzy, her eyes shining.

Miss Damps could hardly believe it. She took off the old cardigan and dropped it into Popeye's basket. He sat down on it at once and made little snarling sounds. The new cardigan fitted beautifully and Miss Damps said because it was purple it made her feel like Queen Elizabeth.

"And the pockets will take lots of apples and biscuits and… hallo somebody has left something in one of them. Perhaps it's a ten shilling note…"

But it was better than that. It was ten clothing coupons. Neither Lizzy nor Miss Damps could believe their luck. They stared at each other.

"As we get forty four coupons a year, that's nearly three months worth," said Miss Damps, working it out on her fingers. "Well, Lizzy now it's my turn! I'm going to buy *you* a present. A really pretty blouse. If we hurry we can just catch the bus…"

The bus roared and rattled its way along the twisting lane which was quite empty apart from an Army convoy of lorries rumbling past at the crossroads.

"Going to that new Army Camp near the Downs. Only it's supposed to be secret," Miss Damps said in Lizzy's ear. The little town was fairly empty too which was just as well as it was to turn out. Lizzy and Miss Damps saw exactly what they wanted in the one and only draper's shop. There weren't many clothes for sale and Lizzy fell in love at once with the blue blouse with white spots. It cost five shillings and eleven pence and the assistant folded it carefully and put it in Damps' basket.

"Thank you," said Lizzy. "It's beaut..." and then she stopped. She and Damps were on the pavement just outside the shop.

There were two bicycles propped up against the curb and further down the street a couple of soldiers were talking to each other. A black cat was strolling across the road and Popeye was starting to snarl at it when everybody went quiet. There was the most extraordinary noise coming out of the still, blue sky. A kind of terrible rumbling, thundering roar like nothing Damps and Lizzie had ever heard before.

They stood and stared upwards, unable to move and then over the rooftops appeared a great black shape with two stubby fins. It was about the size of a fighter plane, but there was no pilot or propeller or wings. It was like some hideous monster and the rumble grew worse...

Suddenly one of the soldiers began to wave his arms and he shouted as loudly as he could.

"It's a buzz bomb, TAKE COVER, TAKE COVER…"

Miss Damps, Lizzy and Popeye dived into a small alley at the side of the shop and crouched down on their hands and knees, Lizzy and Miss Damps with their arms round each other.

And then, quite suddenly, the rumbling, thundering roar stopped. The buzz bomb had vanished towards the meadows and there was absolute silence.

"Well I never saw anything like it before..." began Miss Damps and then her voice was drowned by the most tremendous BANG!

Everything shook and trembled, there
was a steady tinkle of broken glass as
every window in the High Street
shattered. A clang, clang and the two
bicycles fell over and a series of small
crashes as chimney pots and slates fell
off roofs. And then silence again.
"You all right, lady?" it was one of the
soldiers. He helped them to their feet.
"Yes thank you," said Miss Damps shakily.
"Thank you for warning us."

"I've seen 'em a couple of times before," said the soldier. "We say that as long as you can hear the engine cut out you're safe. They glide quite a way after that and *then* they blow up. Tell you what, we could give you a lift in our lorry. I'm sure the Sarge wouldn't mind..."

Which is how Miss Damps and Lizzy, still rather shaken and decidedly dusty, arrived home in the back of an army lorry. Lizzy had perked up, but Miss Damps was still rather pale as they were helped down at the garden gate.

But this wasn't the end of a most unusual day.
Miss Damps' front door was thrown open and
down the garden path ran Lizzy's mother and
behind was a tall, deeply tanned and very thin
man in uniform. He and Lizzy looked at each
other and then Lizzy shouted.

"It's my Daddy, it's my Daddy. He's come
home…"

And then, of course, everybody began talking
at once while Popeye barked so hard all four
paws came off the ground.

Chapter Four

Lizzy didn't really know quite what was
happening. Somehow there were five of them
crammed into Miss Damps' kitchen. Lizzy and
her mother were sitting on either side of Lizzy's
father and opposite were Miss Damps and old
Albert who had just turned up with an enormous
bone for Popeye. Everybody was smiling and
talking except for Popeye who was growling with
delight.

Lizzy remembered her father perfectly now.
But she was holding firmly onto his sleeve just in
case he vanished again while he told them about
his adventures. He told how he had been taken
prisoner in Italy and then how he'd escaped and
hidden with the Italian partisans, or resistance
army, in the mountains – and how they had never
had quite enough to eat. As he was just having
his third slice of bread with Miss Damps' chewy
jam it showed that you could eat anything if you
were hungry enough.

"Dear me!" said Miss
Damps, jumping to her feet.
"I nearly forgot your Surprise
Prize, Lizzy!"

Lizzy looked at the banana
doubtfully. There have been
so many surprises today. She took off the peel
and then asked her mother if she would like some
of it. But she shook her head.

"It's *your* prize, Lizzy. But perhaps Daddy...?"

Lizzy cut the banana in two and gave half to
her father while the other three watched them. To
Lizzy's astonishment it was *delicious*. She could
have eaten five of them.

"Thank you, Lizzy," said her father, "that was practically my best surprise too. One day when the war's over we'll buy a bunch of bananas every week, but until then we'll just have to whistle for them..."

Lizzy beamed at him.

"Will you teach *me* to whistle? I can nearly, *nearly* do it..."

She didn't know why everybody was laughing. But it didn't matter, they were all together and having a wonderful time. Lizzy screwed up her face, pursed up her mouth and blew. And very, *very*, nearly whistled...

Another title by Elisabeth Beresford from Hodder Children's Books . . .

THE FIRST EXCITING STORY ABOUT LIZZY:

Lizzy's War
Illustrated by James Mayhew

One moment it was just an ordinary Saturday afternoon and the next . . .

After her house is destroyed by a bomb, Lizzy goes to stay
with old Miss Damps, who is very kind and great fun.
They soon become the best of friends. There's more freedom
and fun to be had in the country . . . but the hardships and dangers
of war are never far away, as Lizzy and Miss Damps discover.

The Shoemaker's Boy
Written by Joan Aiken
Illustrated by Alan Marks

"I have come to ask a favour of you . . ."

It is a night for visitors for Jem, the shoemaker's boy,
working alone in his father's famous shop. First, three strange
green children ask him for a set of silver keys, which he knows
nothing about. Then a black knight comes requesting a fine pair
of boots – and also asks for keys. But the third visitor proves to
be the strangest – and most magical – of them all . . .

The King in the Forest
Written by Michael Morpurgo
Illustrated by Tony Kerins

Something was moving at the edge of the forest, something white and small.

As a boy, Tod saves the small white fawn from certain death at
the hands of the King's huntsmen. Tod and the fawn grow up
together, until the fawn becomes a fine, white stag, and leaves,
to become the "King in the Forest". But no kingdom can have
two kings. Will Tod's devotion to his boyhood friend prove strong
enough to save his life once more?